D0934243

A Sister

First Edition
06 05 04 03 02   5 4 3 2 1

Published by
Gibbs Smith, Publisher
P.O. Box 667
Layton, Utah 84041

Order toll-free: (1-800) 748-5439
www.gibbs-smith.com

Edited by Suzanne Taylor
Designed and produced by J. Scott Knudsen, Park City, Utah
Printed and bound in Hong Kong

Library of Congress Cataloging-in-Publication Data

Pearson, Carol Lynn.
   A Sister : a fable for our times / by Carol Lynn
Pearson; illustrated by Kathleen Peterson.—1st ed.
      p. cm.
ISBN 1-58685-099-7
1. Sisters—Fiction. I. Title.
PS3566.E227 S57 2002
813'.54—dc21
                          2001004918

A Sister

a fable for our times

Carol Lynn Pearson

ILLUSTRATED BY

Kathleen Peterson

Gibbs Smith, Publisher

For Carol Lynn's sister Marie
and
Kathleen's sisters Shauna and Cindy

Fashioned by God just for us, and for whom we are deeply grateful.

And the Woman who had been created in the Garden spoke to God, saying, "And still I am lonely."

"Lonely?" inquired God. "In this splendid garden teeming with life, with herbs and grass and all manner of trees yielding fruit after their kind? With the beasts of the field and fowls of the air? You are lonely?"

"Well, yes," replied the Woman. "I have had hamsters, parakeets, numerous cats and dogs and that goldfish I won in kindergarten. I am grateful for my houseplants and the lilacs out front, the oak trees and mighty redwoods. And still I am lonely."

"But the Man that shares the Garden with you," asked God, "Is he not wonderful, handsome, strong, kind and loving, and does he not adore you?"

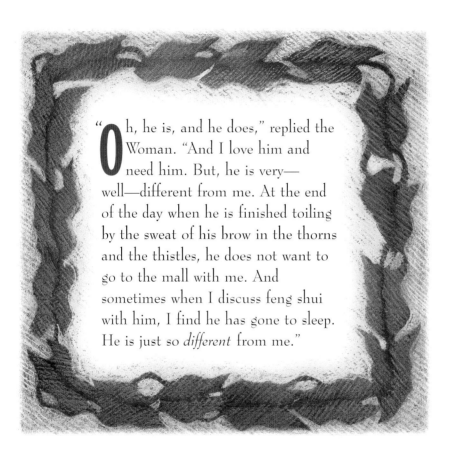

"Oh, he is, and he does," replied the Woman. "And I love him and need him. But, he is very—well—different from me. At the end of the day when he is finished toiling by the sweat of his brow in the thorns and the thistles, he does not want to go to the mall with me. And sometimes when I discuss feng shui with him, I find he has gone to sleep. He is just so *different* from me."

"**H**mmmm," puzzled God thoughtfully. "And the children that I gave you? With them playing at your feet you find yourself still lonely?"

The Woman bowed her head, and spoke with a touch of shame. "Oh, I know they should fulfill all my needs, but even after a day filled with preschool and car pools and corn dogs and homemade juice popsicles and bubble blowing and Nintendo, there is still something missing. Darling as they are, they really don't understand me, you know, and I'm especially worried

about the older one, who is a tiller of the ground. He is growing rowdy and is very mean to his younger brother who is a keeper of the sheep, and I wish I had someone to talk to about theories of discipline."

"Someone like—?" asked God. "Could you be more specific?"

"Well, like—like *me!*" said the Woman. "Let me show you."

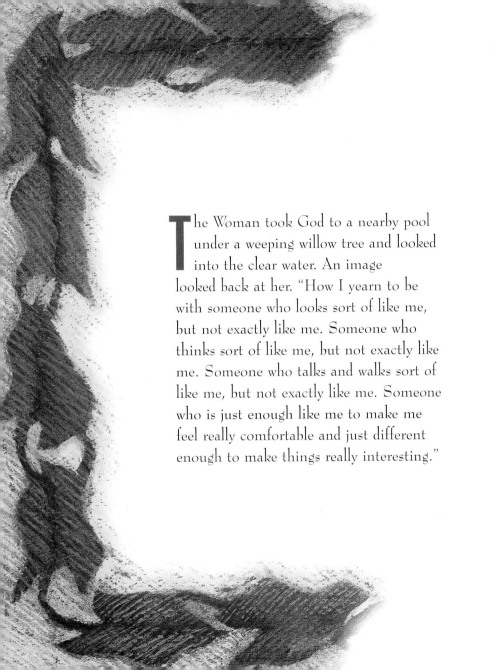

The Woman took God to a nearby pool under a weeping willow tree and looked into the clear water. An image looked back at her. "How I yearn to be with someone who looks sort of like me, but not exactly like me. Someone who thinks sort of like me, but not exactly like me. Someone who talks and walks sort of like me, but not exactly like me. Someone who is just enough like me to make me feel really comfortable and just different enough to make things really interesting."

"Ah!" said God, contemplating the image in the pool. "I understand!" And then God troubled the water with a divine finger. The image rippled into a new form, one that looked sort of like the Woman, but not exactly.

"What is this?" asked the Woman in amazement.

"I think I will call it a Sister," said God. "Yes, a Sister. She is made in my likeness and in yours, after my image and yours. She's something like what I had in mind to create down the road as a Friend."

"What is a Friend?" asked the Woman.

"Sort of like a Sister," said God, "only not as good."

The hand of God scooped the new image from the pool and poured her before the astonished Woman.

"Does she speak?" asked the Woman hopefully.

"Love your fig leaves," said the Sister, "but don't you think it would look cuter if . . ."

The Woman squealed and threw her arms out wide to her Sister. "Yes! Yes! This is *exactly* what I had in mind!"

The Woman and her Sister embraced, and God smiled.

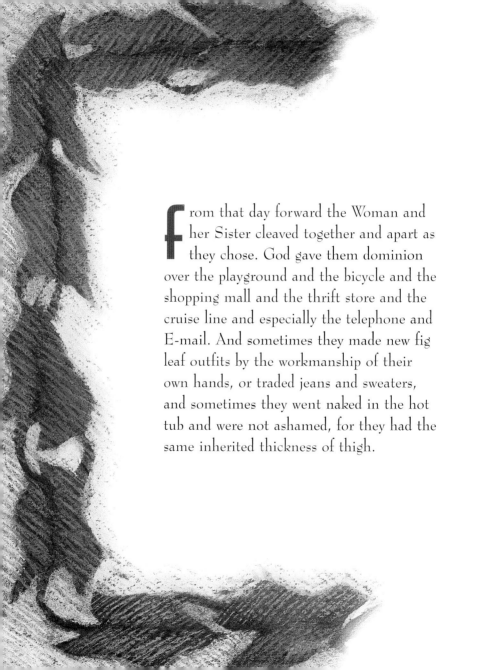

from that day forward the Woman and her Sister cleaved together and apart as they chose. God gave them dominion over the playground and the bicycle and the shopping mall and the thrift store and the cruise line and especially the telephone and E-mail. And sometimes they made new fig leaf outfits by the workmanship of their own hands, or traded jeans and sweaters, and sometimes they went naked in the hot tub and were not ashamed, for they had the same inherited thickness of thigh.

Sometimes the Woman and her Sister quarreled or tattled or were bossy or ignored each other, and sometimes they put a strip of tape down the center of their room. But when one needed a quarter, the other was the first to give it. And woe to the person who harmed or insulted the one, for the other was a fearsome defender. More often than not, they could be found giggling or whispering, and never again was the Woman heard to complain of being lonely.

The entire Garden was blessed by the presence of the Sister. The Man was blessed because the Woman sang more and had someone else with whom to discuss feng shui.

The Woman's children were blessed because they had an Aunt to remember their birthdays and take them to Disneyland, and to demonstrate to the tiller of the soil and the keeper of the sheep that there were peaceable ways to solve problems.

The beasts of the field and fowls of the air and the trees and herbs were blessed because the Woman and her Sister watered the flowers together, and were very attentive to conservation of energy and recycling of plastics, and with love they protected the rain forest.

All the days of their lives the Woman and her Sister walked together. And when the eyesight of the one began to fail, the other read the menu, speaking the words clearly. And when the one stumbled and broke a hip, the other was there at her bedside, spooning in applesauce and showing photographs of when they were small.

One day, as a resting place was being prepared for the Sister, near the pool and under the weeping willow, God spoke to the Woman, saying, "I think I forgot something. This Sister that I created— I pronounce her good."

The woman brushed the hair that was now white and thin and grew in a cowlick over the right temple very much like her own did. "Yes," she smiled—

"Very, very good."